BOOKS BY KENNETH KOCH

Poetry
Poems
Ko, or A Season on Earth
Permanently
Thank You and Other Poems
When the Sun Tries to Go On
The Pleasures of Peace
The Art of Love
The Duplications
The Burning Mystery Of Anna
    in 1951
Days and Nights
Selected Poems: 1950–1982

Fiction
Interlocking Lives
The Red Robins

Theater
Bertha and Other Plays
A Change of Hearts:
    Plays, Films, and Other Dramatic Works
The Red Robins

Educational Works
Wishes, Lies, and Dreams:
    Teaching Children to Write Poetry
Rose, Where Did You Get That Red?:
    Teaching Great Poetry to Children
I Never Told Anybody:
    Teaching Poetry Writing in a Nursing Home
Sleeping on the Wing:
    An Anthology of Modern Poetry (*with Kate Farrell*)

On the Edge

Edge

P O E M S   B Y

KENNETH KOCH

ELISABETH SIFTON BOOKS

VIKING

ELISABETH SIFTON BOOKS · VIKING
Viking Penguin Inc., 40 West 23rd Street,
New York, New York 10010, U.S.A.
Penguin Books Ltd, Harmondsworth, Middlesex, England
Penguin Books Australia Ltd, Ringwood, Victoria, Australia
Penguin Books Canada Limited, 2801 John Street,
Markham, Ontario, Canada L3R 1B4
Penguin Books (N.Z.) Ltd, 182–190 Wairau Road,
Auckland 10, New Zealand

First published in simultaneous hardcover and paperback editions by
Viking Penguin Inc. 1986
Published simultaneously in Canada

William Carlos Williams, *Collected Later Poems*, © 1948 by William Carlos
Williams. Reprinted by permission of New Directions
Publishing Corporation.

Portions of the poem "Impressions of Africa" first appeared, sometimes in a
slightly different form, in *Boulevard, The New York Review of Books, The Poetry
Project Newsletter*, and *Raritan*.

LIBRARY OF CONGRESS CATALOGING IN PUBLICATION DATA
Koch, Kenneth
  On the edge.
  "Elisabeth Sifton books."
  I. Title.
PS3521.O27O48   1986   811'.54   85-40565
ISBN 0-670-80939-X

Printed in the United States of America by
R. R. Donnelley & Sons Company, Harrisonburg, Virginia
Set in Bulmer

In memory of my mother,
Lillian Loth Koch
1897–1983

Acknowledgments

I am indebted to Kate Farrell for her editorial assistance with these—and other—poems, for which I thank her very much. For help in my travels in Africa, I should like to thank Jean-Marc Rolland, Holly Stewart, Will Sutter, and Kate Delaney, Robert Palmeri, and others of the A. R. S. in Paris.

CONTENTS

IMPRESSIONS OF AFRICA

The back roads, if there are back roads
Have gone to sleep
Daggers have coughs on them
And quoits have cures
And doors have racking heat
The sciences have beds with fevers.

1. MADAGASCAR. SUBCONTINENT

In the Hotel Colbert, pronounced Coal-Bear
In the bar
I saw a big, pretty girl who looked like Lisa
Behold a magazine a new life of women is about to appear
I sat at my *chocolat* writing
The sea-bird inviting
And the Lisa-looking girl didn't smile or even look
At me but soon she got out of there
And she went walking
Down the sidewalk-colored street not thinking of me
Lisa-looking girl, come back!
Give me or don't give me a little bit of ecstasy
Help me to find the answer
How long does life last?

The Académie Malgache
Is nothing
Wearing my new pink suit
Is nothing
Wishing you were there
Is nothing
But nothing helps me out
It helps me to see the lemurs
In the pre- and post-restaurant air

And in the time before I slide around in fear
On the floor in a nightmare
Which didn't happen in fact
At the Hotel Colbert.

Change my room!
The fourteen-year-old
Girl still a young
Flower not yet
Into the age
Of her race
And all characteristics
Mops the fields
With her hair
In long tresses are
They women, other, wear
Green and orange dresses
A man holding a rake
Something
To duel with a rice
Paddy? or other field.

Where will it all end?
In the Market, around this bend
As I go down, my feet go down with me
People are sitting lying standing end to end.

To be exploding, like a fiddle, outside of myself
I am thinking on yellow roads of Madagascar
I have been there
Like a bird on a shell
Or like the mountain coming down over that
Sun sea shelf

And like the chair yellow and pink and red
That exists only in the head
At the side of the sea shell, in Madagascar

Which is not Africa, some say,
It breaks away from Africa, just in time
To preserve the lemurs
A few hours later
The lions came down
And the apes came down
From a bend at the top of Africa
Rushed there by the climate
Knowing it can't last
Neither did Africa, Madagascar
Left it, storm of red,
Blue, yellow
And rice paddies
And villages with stone tombs left it
With Polynesians coming to it left it
And with the stone booths
And the climatic exchange.

The Earthly Paradise—"Wait till I get there!"
Once in Antananarivo, however, it seemed too far away
(Forty kilometers by sea) and to take too long to get there.
This island, drenched by perfume fragrances, boasts many cabanas,
With paradise—where? A woman in Paris
Told me about it. Ah!
You are going to my country! there you will
Find the paradise—an island
That smells so sweetly
They have the perfume-bearing trees that it is called
Paradise, or Perfume Island.
But in Gaboon, as in Zaire, they said when you get there
Communist-government-ruined, ah you are

Going to Madagascar! I had a fine, confused state
Of mind about this subcontinental island state
An East-Berlin gray broken-up boulevard mist
Ambiance, and le paradis terrestre.

Tanarive centrale, there is a lake
So choked with waterlilies
That you would not believe
It was not planned to be that way, to take
You by the throat by its sudden beauty—unexpected, boaty,
And plain—but then you can see
It's a little messed-up and goaty
Around the edges, after which it doesn't look the same
When you drive by it on your way to the intersections.

In varied patterns you see them they vary
And they are patterned
Of the crops in the fields
And the clothes of the men
And the women and children
In varying colors, patterns
The automobile running
It used to be a paradise
Flesh but with unusual graces and with a "soul."

Dixebat Julie—nom correcte? mot juste?
O Malagasy plumes! In the market so used
Sumptuousness! She said (did) words
Madagascar we feel thrown, we feel the thrown
Stone one out here in the sea (she)
(Didn't) (say it). I thought
It, while she was going around
And around helping me to buy jewelry, it was

Getting dark, in the market. Here is a good stone,
Says she, and a good price, too, I get on this one!

So much closer to me
By big civilization compared
To walkings of Brazza
And even than the poets there!
In a certain sense.
Old hotel—of innocence.
Gare Centrale—mammary of competence.
And nerves under the hat.

Hard to get out of the restaurant
Hard to stand up from the table and pay
Hard to move quickly enough
Through the arbiters gentlemen
Unthreatening who have rather
The mild excitingness which travel
Gives to the un-noteworthy like a gun.

Standing around
The water fountain
Fifteen girls
Or maybe ten
Look at him
Then look away
Nothing happens
On this day
In the village of Ankazobe.

Evenings in Madagascar
It used to be a paradise

According to the French
In a memorial unitary
Naval military
Dotting up of times.

The huge tombstones
Are a traveler's bust—
Finally, Antony's bust is not like Antonina's!
The white cool stones on the path
On the way up to the Queen's hut
Say so again and again and again—
Go out to dinner. Inside, no lights.

The Queen had her own swimming pool. No one else was allowed to use it.
And there was a door of the dead, too, as in Gubbio. And a small, special
    room
To which only the royal dead, in their coffins, were ever moved. And this is
    the Royal Door. The whole palace complex was constructed for the
    Queen
Ramabanabamabanjana by a minor British architect
In the style of a Scottish summer lodge, in eighteen-fifty-four.

The clean way
Up to the palace
And the green way
Down. Down under there's a lot of ground
Where roots and insects stay and all around
The lives of the mild, poor people of Madagascar.

Down there, it's shipping
Up here, it's rice.

8

Black is the night sky above the central Madagascar
Plateau on which the capital is situated. Here the climate
Is temperate. There below
Are the steamy rivages where all-Black people dwell,
Malagasy-speakers, although resembling the Continental Africans.

The Malagasy all speak Malagasy, she said
They aren't divided up into different tribes
Speaking Tangasy and Longasy and Fugasy
But Malagasy everywhere you walk or drive
Even into the deepest and most remote place.

With its cruel mask of domination taken off
France offers, among the nations, too beautiful a face
Not to have a choice spot
In every free man's heart
Said Jacques Rabemananjara. He drank the rice water.
The French officers drank wine. Are these officers the Presence
France genuinely wants to have in Mad-
Agascar? "The whole problem is there," said Jacques,
The problem of every far-from-the-center action,
Of every far-from-the-center place.

It is a plain faucet
The day goes by
Water! streams out of it
I had thought, A spring, maybe, but
Reality
Has other ideas
Today appearing to me
At Ankazobe with its fifteen girls
Sunset sunrise days go by still
Is there a still center where desire

Is not American enthusiasm, where it is a rushing-
Forward ball of diamond flickers, as
At Ankazobe? Oh, the cloth sleeve on her arm
As she puts it forward to hold a bucket under the swash
Or "gold it under" when the sun comes out,
Of the, for me, as I watch from this distance, soundless water!

Forgetting four months
Going back to a time
When it was powerful
The early morning sun once again picks up
The bare outlines of some straw.

Across the river
First the blacksmith
Then the market. Forging a heel of steelness
He's making horseshoes, he crafts the dullness
Of raw shapeless matter into a thing
That has a ring; he also makes the frame of a bed.

Purple, yellow, and red
Clothes, to make her forget
She is not supposed
To be totally interested in that.
It's just cloth made and dyed and cut
And draped around the human butt
Of Amédie Amenangala
On the way to Amatafy.

Everything naturalizes into on-the-way
Purple and yellow in the eyes' way
Give up!

Whatever you find out traveling you don't know
Whatever you find out moving is used up.

An ambiance slightly rah-rah very unlike that in Brah Zah
Invades, evokes, equips this home in Tah Nah
Where to the Malgache night
We send out words of wisdom slightly flawed—
Find the meaning of what I am doing since Zaire?
Maybe—will she?—or not.

Eheu, Madagascar! Closer to home, what?
Not a part of Africa, really, a hot shot
Among African nations, this subcontinent
Basks in the reflected glory
Of the mappemondo's number-one hot spot, the Queen
Of Continents,
Who graciously grants it this blot
In mid-ocean, not far from the un-concreted shores.

In a constant blither-dither of can't-wait-to-get-out
It gets out, and scintillates, and rises, and fights, and flies,
And careens, and ends up, and was a day, of storms and inclusions.

The crowds of lights
At nine o'clock
In Tanarive
Go out.

Soon I will be back in
The clasping-type shoes of the street
Near the there on the banks of

The Central Lake to be looking at
Anticipatable only after a while
Clapboard houses. The winds take
A ten-hour break. No
Shudder of leaf temples at all.

Vincent RIZERIE Rabehaga the rice
Is still being produced here while at the Chocolaterie
Robert, on the same road,
It is shuttered-up windows, and trees
Edging the closed-down factory, where, in other days,
Came truck and car and wagon to remove
The chocolates over the hills to Tanarive.

And Lake Itasy grows nearer
And nearer, and the city of Tana is passed
And soon we are in the outskirts of Ampefy!
Ampefy is a logging town
And a fishing town. Windows of Ampefy
Open to let the Am air in
And the Pef air out, while Y stays still
In Ampefy, "The Broad-Bosomed."

You are perhaps making too much
Of this little trip to Ampefy
And Lake Itasy, during which
Nothing, or just about as close
To nothing as anything can be, happened.
The ruins (remains) of lake architecture.
The big bee
And the red bird. Above and beyond Itasy and Ampefy.

Holly is the embassy attachée. Other personnel
Darkens. She is the cultural

Attachée. This, too, is a cultural attachment,
What happens today.

A silver-haired calligrapher has stolen my storm window
At night I try to sleep
The air conditioner doesn't work, not really
It doesn't bring in the hilly town and its streets
Or the fields and the air that is with them, so I prepare
To get cool in a non-working shower and go downstairs
To the Colbert Bar, ampersand of my nights and days.

A bird is its own balcony—
And so is Madagascar, an annual rain on its head.

As the sun shines, a man
Is making and selling raffia giraffes
Beside the road.
There are no giraffes here. They moved in
To Africa after Madagascar had moved out.

Not because the bed was hot
Or anyone was married
The road ran on, as far as the outskirts of the city
Then it stopped.
They keep
Giving this government money.
Laurel and Hardy and the elephants
Sleep outside.

Holly of the Consulate
Keeps me in the car. She

Talks a lot. A jar
's for sale in Madagascar.
A woman keeps
Her foot on the tan reach
Of the irrigation ditch going over
To the other, less-deep-blue side.

Disturbing to be on the road
Without a car under you, without a card
To identify you, without a car-nail
With which you could make your name on a stone, if you had to.

On my way!
I sit in the Colbert
And think about Zaire.
The Jillian-looking
Girl reminds me of Kenya.
The dot-dot-looking girl
Reminds me of the Hell
Of certain relationships.
Coffee returns me
But the life in the village goes on.
"The true life," they say in Zaire,
"Is the life of the ancestors.
And the true village
Is the village under the ground."

How far from the true voyage
Is the voyage by car? by air?
I think the one
Who looks like Jillian
May be a whore. She reads
The newspaper. Legs.

The true woman
Is the woman at the bar
As well as the woman she resembles.
The true bar is the one with great umbrellas
Sweeping over seven hundred miles of ground,
Flowing, and bringing no snowflakes down, through Africa.

The thing about Madagascar,
I try to explain, sitting
With no one to
Talk to but myself
While
The "boot" part
Of day escapes—five to
Six-thirty p.m.—is that it seems
More like France, more
Like what I'm used to, thus
I'm more "myself" (I say
To myself) in the
Rather "advanced," mixed-up way
I escaped in the rest of Africa
Because it was so hard.

The capital of Madagascar has streets
One can walk around in at night, although
It does not have many street lamps. Also there is hardly
Any place public to go. When the French
Were here, the streetways were ignited
With places to eat and drink and dance, and
Possibly, even to find romance, to go from the ball
With someone you have met, into the Malagasy night. Now
Darker, and emptier, it seems country enough so that
In it you don't necessarily forget
The outskirts, with their darker streets

Or the mountains (very high
Hills, anyway) with their trees.

Rice fields are not giving any water
To the gin drinkers seated with some daughters
At the Pousse Café. Besides which, a rice
Shortage is under way. Honk! says Bumbudun of
The Embassy. And the Marines came
At night. I saw them sitting
With their shaved crowns in the way
Of the filigree atop the Bar. And then again at the airport
I saw them, like God's American Swollen Ping-Pong-Ball Heads on
    Holiday. Can you imagine
IMPORTING rice to this country? From this embassy irony a way
's found to the rice water, Malgache specialty, consisting
Of warm water, relatively, in which has been cooked rice.
You drink it, swinging your eyes away to
The field daughters, and others, going home, baskets on heads.

2. SENEGAL. PORT

Keep your courage up
Walk down the street
When the leper comes up to you
Say I am a Moslem
And give him a franc
Soon he will be carted away
By the Department of l'Encombrement Humain.

Go to the Island of the Slaves
On Sunday, said the Black cultural attaché, who speeded me
Down hallways through consular doorways
Then suddenly back out onto the street.
At five o'clock everything closes
Or did he say one o'clock or two or three or four o'clock?
In any case, everything is closed
But I find someone to talk to in a building (mauve)
Past the horse (white).

A young man, tall (high, rather)
And skilled at walking fast
And with his head on high comes past
At an amazing angle and an amazing rate.

Fashions change slowly. And
Books rarely have an influence
Because few people read them. No one speaks about
The pattern of the young men walking
Bisecting and trisecting each other's striding poles
Backwards and frontways hand-arm waving
Beneath palms, on the Place de l'Indépendance.

Don't go to the bars, Jean-Marc said, and try
To talk to the girls. This one is OFF LIMITS. This one is
OFF LIMITS. I am ON LIMITS with my arms. Why that man
Stuck with a tooth stick? The Lebanese
Men go there, with their sisters
They start to fight if you talk to or touch one.

"The Russians in Dakar Harbor are not allowed
To get off their ship for fear that they will
Be seduced by capitalism," he said. "It's the truth!"

In Dakar you are still pretty close to Europe
But three miles out of town you are burning in a pink lake
Unless you get out of it fast with your modicum of salt.
These modicums grown additive on the lake banks
Show white and fair to a far-off who views them but
Up near, they stink. And the salt lake burns you. And, Dad,
I am leaving, you do not say if you are a member of this tribe,
This special tribe of nomads who dredge for salt.

On the boat to Gorée, how cruel
These four Lebanese are, led by this one
Young man who keeps calling to and then laughing at
A Mongoloid (of maybe twenty-five or thirty)—
Laughing at his clumsy gait and at his efforts to please
Them in an absurd and helpless way.

That man on this boat
Looks like Mayakovsky, black—his face
Showing his character and his art,

His violent, virile, and touchingly
Avant-garde, Futurist, lyric poetic art.

Seeds on my head! Sitting under
A baobab. Big, knotty tree—baobab!
You're spreading all over like a Roman or Athenian map!

Everything is wrecked—misery, stoniness, and the color
Of sickness, or dying, is dancing on it all.

Tu as le choc, you have
Ze shock! said Jean-Marc
Aiverybuddy get whan comb to Africa. It goes away.
But it took more than two days going away.
For these two days I hate life, Africa, everything.
Next day, a little better. Three
Weeks later, I am in an enchantment—Kenya!
Madagascar! the sun shock under the place names
Like skin under clothes.

Greater than the shock of the insects of the Congo,
Greater than the clock of Madame N'Zambo's hair.
It's the shock of poor people, desperately poor.
Wanting—everything. Which
In their case is almost nothing. Everything.

The man sweeping the building
After dark is of a higher caste
Than the one who directs the company
And rules it from the topmost floor.
To his air-conditioned office

Suite, comes Eng-al-Baram
And the president bows down.

The slaves were brought in this way
And taken out this way.
Here is where they stood
Waiting for the boat
To take them to America
In chains where they would create
The characters of Darky and Mammy, good slave, bad slave,
Hanged man, mulatto, quadroon, and then would change
To "underprivileged citizens," preachers, doctors—
Violent transformations, while
Africa stayed here all along,
Visited by rainfall and heat spells,
With a different kind of energy and a different kind of change.

The partition of Africa takes place
In eighteenth- and nineteenth-century
Europe, on conference tables. Here is the place
Where one Oolof will wear a beret, and the other a bush hat,
Where one will drink wine, and the other feel lost without his tea.

In Dakar at night
Léopold Sédar Senghor is sitting and thinking
Just as Wallace Stevens might have wanted him to—
But he finds he is not thinking right.
He eats some moospasla and goes to sleep.

Blue, brave
Flash of the ocean's
Water, like a screen

Through which I see
The street, the streets,
The teeming, busy,
Commercial, African,
Impoverished, beggar—
Filled, lavish, horrible
Streets of Dakar
The city's been left ajar
Fortunately so that the breeze
Can come in, although Islam
And the rest of Dakar
Don't go out.

Senghor was President.
Poets here are residents, too.
Fleeing from Haiti
Jean Brière (and others) found a free literary haven in Dakar.

Oh the part that's by the ocean that's
Fine, says Jean-Marc. The part that you see.
But in the rest of the country it's horrible—
There's no water, dried out, death to the economy!

I am like a shark at the reef
Said King Behanzu, upon hearing
That the French were debarking at Catarou.
And he delayed them but he could not stay them.
Of King Behanzu's defense there remains a statue
Of King Behanzu as a shark—"At the Reef."

3. GABOON. COAST

As in Gaboon, the white road jumps past the hospital
Up to the sun-
Drenched French bathing suit companies of half-
Naked women who don't ask me along
As if I saw the moon, entirely, one
Body, from an air-conditioned room. The young woman speaks
French, lying on her back, her breasts
Bare, in the hotel pool.

The Malaria doctor. "I implore you!" Steepness.
Millions of pieces of junk on the street,
And dirt. I'll take a walk.
And now it's raining
Again. Jean-Guy takes me
To the "village of sculptors" where
I look at nothing for a while.

Tell me, the young sculptor
Is covered with dust, Raconte-moi,
Chef, ce que c'est que la littérature française.
On en parle mais je ne comprends pas. Well, literature, I said,
Is made up of poetry, fiction, and plays. French literature is
    all of that
In the French language. Oh is that it? he said.
C'est cela! Ça alors je ne savais pas!

Dust is flying everywhere
In this half-commercial half-traditional industry
Center, this tiny village, where, I would say,
The heads they make are more half-bad than half-good.
The sculptors have a careful but, finally, a nonchalant

Attitude toward what they are doing. It
Comes out right, it comes out right. No
Question, it seems, of a "break-through,"
Of a new artistic conception of the nature of the human head.

Préfères-tu Senghor ou Césaire? he said. Césaire,
I said. Ah, si. Oui. Moi aussi. He puts down his chisel. Oui,
   toi tu as raison.

Négritude. A Black world. Black consciousness. What
A splendid idea Aimé Césaire had, for writing poems
And for breaking through the light with something to say,
With days on the calendar, every day an estimate if right
Or wrong the négritude and with and when, and a way of talking.
Négritude contre la fièvre du monde blanc, as I take Lanaquil
Contre le paludisme, indigenous to these parks
And valleys that vanish as you sit in them or walk through the mirage
Till Mama Africa becomes Boum boum boum!

The horizon's always rounder near the Equator.
O Hotel Rapontchombo elevator
Where I may meet the bare breasts of Gaboon!
But I don't. I rarely leave my room
But sit around and think of "Rapontchombo"
What does it mean in Fang? Jean-Pierre is downstairs.
I bang into the elevator. There's a casino
In this hotel, off-limits to the Gabonese. All the meat
And vegetables come from France. I see an old woman,
She looks likeable—and real. She, too, is probably imported.
It's the sunlight of Gaboon, the horizon-rounding equator
And the rising and sinking pontoon of the hotel elevator!

Difficult, says Jean-Pierre, to meet the *indigènes.* I don't
Manage to do it, except for Jacques Rupombo and Helène
Desforêts, the only Gabonese novelist, who, when
We appear together on television, shares with me the sweet oxygen
Of the indoors functioning air-conditioning of Gaboon.
Although it is very hot under those lights she says
Kind things. Jacques Rupombo says, "The world has need . . ."
And other lively exaggerations, and I don't know anything
More about the people than I did when I came in-
To the country.

Glamorous she is, in a Gabonese manner,
But she doesn't write well, one of the Frenchmen says—
I couldn't read her novel, my copy of it
Falls a short, sandy, humid distance to the
Floor of Room One Thousand and Sixty-Six
In the Hotel Rapontchombo, from where I pick it up
Later, it may not be her fault that I can't
Read it, there is my sleepiness, my dissatisfaction,
My stomach trouble here in Gaboon! I still
Have read only one sentence of the book and I
Am being picked up in five minutes by Buroombo
To be driven to the airport. What should I do? It's
Heavy, I carry it with me.

Today there is XY of the Embassy and the exorbitant structures
That constitute the Presidential Palace of Bongo, Omar
El Haij, President of Gaboon, whom the little gray French airfield
Is keeping in power. He, being from a very small tribe,
Not one of the big ones, can govern equably
And keep the French language and keep calm the Fang,

Relatively speaking. A little bomb is thrown now
And then, into the miles of avenue lizard shit in this
Sulky "Paris by the sea" as someone described it
To me in Paris, so I thought I would go there, come here,
I'm not sorry I did, but it's confusing,
As Nice would be if it were filled with lizards and all
The food you ate and every thought you had
Were brought in from thousands of miles away.

Madame Ounala's
Breasts in the Rapontchombo Hotel
And her beguiling smile
Madame Ounala, who
Is not half-Christian and half-Jew
But half-French and half-Gabonese
Whose beauty makes my knees
Shiver of the Rapontchombo Hotel
Desk area quiver a white seat
Cushion's inviting
Over there somebody sits
On it gives me the key
To my "deposit box" (*dépot*). Her dress, upper
Dress, moves, as it
Comes only with such swelling breasts
To move—I will never get this woman to my bed.
Perhaps I can manage to have her speak to me
In a somewhat less impersonal way.

A man in a big suit comes to see Madame Ounala
And he must be her husband or her lover with a stolen
Happiness right in the middle of his life
While the sea birds are watching, in Gaboon.

The French in Gaboon, in Saint
Louis, deliberately created
A future native ruling class, as
Follows: the French men married
Gabonese women. The half-
French half-Gabonese children
Were to rule and be happy in Gaboon
But things turned out differently.

At the university, Madame Hua informs me,
It's the country kids who write the best French,
The children from the bush. All of one tribe
In the village, they speak the language of the tribe, and French
Is only for school. In Libreville, however,
Of different tribes, they have to speak French
Or not speak at all, and
It is imperfect, of course, full of errors, and not pure.

The *Mvett*'s a Gaboon (Fang) oral epic written down in French
And the best of Gaboon literature, if the very central essence of Gaboon
Is what you're after, it's what I'm after, I read the *Mvett*
Which is full of exclamation, singing, and exaggeration.
The hero sets out to destroy all the iron on the earth
Because iron is the cause of all sorrow—discord, war, and death.

The two members of the "Party," wearing Omar Bongo shirts,
Looked neither humorous nor arty, and that they were flirts
Wasn't something anyone would think of. For them, life's just deserts
It seemed were their ongoing roles in the national Party
Enclosing all beauty, strength, ideas, everything that's best.

They abjure the Gabonese people to work hard each day.
"It is as a bird that is fallen from the mother bird's nest
When one of you does not," says Thin Sad Eye, while Big Fat
Guy spears at his notes, and says: "Each day that you don't
Work for Gaboon it is like a wound that you are giving to your country's
    body."

Light flashes on palm trees
Mosquitoes go around
Toward the casino.
His name was not
Omar until his conversion to
Islam a short time ago.

We live only for our vacations, said the *coopérant*, co-operator,
And four of them said they would phone me in Paris and didn't.
They live at the University,
How end, how start! And there are just no books
Says the Prof. de la Littérature Américaine. He reads to his students out
    loud.
Their favorite American writer is Ambrose Bierce.

"You have made me," the man in the beard said, "vibrate!
I once wrote poems. Then I stopped. To hear
Those poems you read," he said, "though, made me vibrate
Again and I wished to write again, which I may, and vibrate."
Trans.: Tu m'as fait vibrer. The driveway stone-white in the tropical flat car
    skimmed
To a stop. Heavy the heat fell over the
Ocean, even. A jar could have held all our thoughts.

I sit what seems forever in this room
Thinking over and over, I am in Gaboon.

The ocean out there is dark.
I feel imprisoned, as in a Noah's Ark
Of which I'm the poetical baboon.

France is still here. Here's their
Military airport. They keep
Bongo in power, I hear,
To prevent the accession of the Fang
Who'd stamp their language on the land of Gaboon
And zap the leaders of the other tribes, and bang!
The French might be out the door, the
French language out the door, but this
Is extraordinarily unlikely
Since there is uranium in Gaboon.

Yes there's a kind of nullness
A superficial supernatural dullness
A nothing no-place-ness of which I am acquiring a sense
Here in Gab-, Gab-, Gab-, Gabon, Gaboon.

Better it should happen here than someplace else
Where everything always meant something:
The shock (renewed) and being sick. Nulness.
Ahead lies the Heart of Africa, and the East
Of Africa, island with animals, and the doubloon
Of the Pacific, Madagascar, the "Sea Eater."

The stirring
Dust makes
Lizards jump a
Wave comes
In from above

Rapont
Chombo place the
Forest is two
Kilometers away
Face there isn't any
Stomach-ache Ptchombo
Rap on, rap on
All the day Tchombo
Engong did away
With the bad parts
Of Ndoumou Obame
His too much power until
At the end a
Swallow flew out of his
Nostril and flew by
The People
In the separate
Villages a great bright
Light engulfed the earth and
No one could see.

There are forty-seven languages in Gaboon!
Or forty-eight. And it was here that Dr. Schweitzer worked in his hospital
On steaming-horrid summer days chasing the microbes none too soon
From the fever-battered bodies of the Fang and other tribes of Gaboon.
His hospital is a long way
From Libreville. Saint Louis
Was the capital before that, and before that,
Before the colonists, there was not even any conception
Of a capital of Gaboon.
People fled from the north and the east, arriving in
The bush, to eat animals, manioc, and each other—the
Fang are cannibals—were. There was only forest then. At Lambaréné,
Where, after, the hospital was, the Effik and Bubu were treated,
And later M'Pongwe and Fang.

4. THE CONGO AND ZAIRE. RIVER

Quoi? said Matila
Sudi (écrivain congolais),
You mean to say
There are poets
In the contemporary U.S.?
Pour nous vous êtes le pays
De Vietnam, de Watergate, et de la bombe hydrogène.

The moon seems floating, high, tonight
Above the frames of Brazza-
Ville in which I arrive after a flight
Through the bedtime air over half of Africa.

Henri says
She came to his room
Ambassador of the Ambassador
All the French stay
Put up lamp posts, little enough
Says Jean-Jacques
(Embassy driver)
For what they've done
The Chinese on the other hand
Build hospitals
("With those people we get along well")
And live simply
Not in expensive houses.

I thought, venereal disease, bankrupt,
Father, mother, stymie, stump,
Stunned. This is where the Russians eat
Imperial Café. At night they sleep at the Cosmos.

Take me round Congo
Three hours all day. Goat side
And head. Merci. Why Henri
To the white-coated consular eventuality deeply thinkingly costlily friendlily
    frostily (by this time
The pamphlets start arriving, F.A.H. enraged, red
Face from auto emerging) said Zaira moosa be-a
Freedom offa Congo. Oltremong
Ze hull world eez een trap. So Unmbala Lavinia Black stopped
Shortly front his hotel door. Now, his head's
On around actually, winking and winked at, somewhere else.

More my village sleeping onward
Into the bush it goes. These fragments
On dead rocks, stone. Animals are chased from here
To make the city. Lilies come floating down. Big river.
Big Congo rushing and going and coming—
Said Michel, I'd make ze treep just for that!

Yes, hope
Springs always in our souls
As we cross the Congo
In search of girls.

Bastards! he said. Stupid
Sons of bitches! Jesus!
These fucking people! Christ!
I said,
How did you happen to get
In the diplomatic service?
He said for Christ's sake

Look at those cocksuckers
Standing in the middle of the road
Fuck! Squeal! go the brakes
Meanwhile Henri
Is photographed
For the Brazzaville *Express*
Standing in his white suit with his hand
On Kronemann's *Legal Briefs and Excise*
"When there is no justice in the Congo,"
Says Henri, "there is no justice
For any man or any woman anywhere!"
Shit-heads! said Deak
Of the Embassy. I asked
Why did you
Choose the diplomatic service, anyway?
Henri escaped
The Authorities. The
Black woman stayed in his bed.

I am perhaps foolish
To stand here just looking
And smiling
And saying Bon jour.

All the same in the middle of life
Some white houses in Brazza
Ah, we were all beautiful
Once she said
And cut them and
Gave them to me in my hand
By William Carlos Williams
Look at the view!
Sturdily through the garbage I seek the view.

Jean-Jacques said, Here are the boats.
One woman out in her pirogue
All alone. Later in the day
There are poets to talk to.
My kiss to you (in a letter—"Dear Z.")
Was the main part
Of this three-to-five-part day
I hear Jean-Jacques honking outside
The black and white of bees
N'Zambo's wife, the Congo, confusion extreme
She keeps
Walking down a "street," until—bush!

Funghi, growing under the bridge—
Eating the very small orange (tangerine?)
And spitting out the seeds. A bird, in its nightgown,
Goes spinning by. I've got to get out of this hotel.
Whole days stretch in seconds and then into minutes.
I do come out, and then—like water!
Smile of someone—I don't have to eat or drink!

And so are oranges, amnesty-like sweet;
Oysters are absent. And
There is no flirting in the Congo! Deak says,
I noticed that—
These god-damned cocksuckers have nothing!
Oooof! Can you imagine balling one of their women?
I imagined, I balled, I paid the rent.
I am the African, I suffragette, iron hair.

A lack of plan. A plan. Chinese men over there,
Governors of the world—"Governors of Paradise,"

"Governors perhaps of nothing, not
Even of their own souls." When I get up next morning and am advised
About which way to walk
I see the sun, silver-white.

I'd better get out of here—shore
I'll put some wings on—flamingo
I don't want to die—by the river
This way to the television station—come on
You're due there at five o'clock—the apples of Tikastra.

Sur les trottoirs de Brazza
Pays where the Com-
Munist government, like all governments, gets fat
But opens up new territory to the Chinese
Who are building the hospitals, I think
Of that (which is not much), while Jean-Jacques
Goes to get something to eat.

"Some, some, some time!" the birds seem to be singing
While there is a tremendous amount of dirt as we pull up.

O television program celebrating the fortieth birthday of *Pravda* (in
    Brazzaville)
Celebrating it as an organ of freedom, how much the dusty streets
Around the azalea bushes reminded him of Norman, Oklahoma,
And how little she thought of anything in the huge dumb station
That was the building inside which was the program that he was on.
First they read the letters—then this celebration of *Pravda*.
D. H. says, "How did it go?" "It went splendid," I cockneyed,
Hearkening back against lamp posts to frail the dust
Cameos against frock-born ceintures Africa seemed heading for my toe.

34

It was an absolute waste of time, I added,
While George Bernard Shaw went on being dead, and Wallace Stevens,
    and the author of *Hernani*
In Brazzaville "la nuit."

I've got to get out of here! I sat
In a big white chair
In the lobby of the Meridien Hotel.
The next day
I got out of there
Or one day after that
Of l'Hotel Meridien.

However, getting out of the Congo is not easy.
You need a pass and transportation and also
"Fucking Bastards" comes along, cursing the natives
But buying me my ticket, finally, so I can get on the boat
Which is taking me to the "Devil's Disneyland," Kinshasa—the Congo
Becoming very, very wide just here.

The wide Congo
Rushing
Trying to get on the boat
The men crippled by polio
In wheelchairs pushing
They get to carry duty-free
Merchandise to
Brazzaville from Kinshasa!
A gift of the Congo's government
To lifelong victims of this disease.

N'Zambo is his name
He hails from the village of M'Gambutenmhumo

He works for the American Embassy
His wife has rigid wires in her hair.

What a huge river
The Congo is!
But if it were named
"The Wink"—
The Congo, or "The Wink,"
Pushing endlessly down toward the Atlantic.

At the dock, boys,
Men, women, old
Men, old women, even,
Fighting to get at something, or someone,
With the city of Kinshasa behind them,
Ten or fifteen times a day.

Hoongam! says N'Zambo and he takes my briefcase
And leaves it on a shelf where Customs won't throw it away.

In Kinshasa the head
Of the driver. In the village the abdomen and the legs.
In the dog, bark.

The Zairian poets, in Kinshasa, were very good-natured and smart.
Romance seemed to play a relatively small role, I thought, in their art.
To get a book published in Kinshasa, you have to
Publish it privately or have a Catholic or Protestant mission house do
It, but you may have trouble if it is violent, sexy, or if you are a Jew,
The latter not being the case with most poets of Zaire
Who tend to mix Victor Hugo

And African drum-repetition types of sounds and to
Write works that sometimes seem to me aesthetically unclear.

In Kin-
Shasa at the
Cultural at-
Taché's place
I
Said to Su-
Maili of
Zaire: Where
Are your
Older writers? Ha!
He said,
Tomorrow
You are going
To see them
And I did
One (the young-
Est of them)
Was only
Forty-five years
Old. But why are they the old ones? Why
Are they the old ones? Because
Of publishing before l'Indépendance.
They are, he said, les Vieux!

With a big country around him
And a lot of other writers around him
A life behind him
And a life ahead of him
Odd to talk to, as if we were going slantways
Or sideways
But I like Sumaili of Zaire

Though neither of us may know (ever)
In fact, what our real "subject" is.

If I set out in my pirogue
And you in yours, we're quite the vogue
Floating on the river, yet we notice
Very, very, very little lettuce
Is being grown on either shore
And there's no magic anymore,
At least none that we know of, on the river,
Which doesn't change the strange way we feel, either,
At daybreak, when a gaggle of flamingo
Starts twisting us to shore.

N'Zambo now comes down to check
If one's to get one's baggage back. Not.

With a big packet of Zaires (the paper money
Of Zaire, which is worthless
Outside of Zaire) you can pay
For your room for one night.
I take off the rubber band
And look out the window
At the dazzling white cars—mostly Renaults.

It is regrettable
Announces the Kinshasa *Soleil*
That a letter
Mailed from Kinshasa
May not be delivered
For up to four weeks
Or four months
Or a year

To someone who is
Living just kilometers away
(In the bush) and so
This newspaper
Warmed by the morning sun
If mailed, may never get to
A reader in Oon-ga-bu-Dun
Before it is uninterestingly out-of-date.

At the Ambassador's house, the flowers are sitting
In glasses on a table. Tonight he is not the host
But some young woman who is crazy about going into the bush
On a small airplane, landing, and settling local disturbances
That stem from the chaotic ungovernability
Of Zaire, made up of so many tribes, with multifold languages and
Three times as many wives (for each man) and they come down
Over the mountains and
Slaughter each other. "I want to do as much of this as I can
While I'm still young—before I'm thirty-five!"

This is—I forget the name. The
Thing the people eat all the time. Without much food value. Cassava
    (manioc).

You bake there—and never did you fill me with desire
Except when you were young, very young—
Fifteen? sixteen?—and
Your breasts! which that day I hold in my hands, then
Marriage, and a mysteriously useful son.

To fundamental questions
Africa me brought. That's what they all like about it. The excitement
And the illusion of living at the beginning of thought.

Even old Rep told me about it. While I napped
He went out riding on his bicycle, into thought!

Now it is time to go
But I can't mark
The place exactly where a chief took down
A mango from a tree and gave extremely
Small boy deadly smiles to me
To other kinds of look.
That one is all.

A smokiness is rising from the fire flakes
Old woman crouching there a hand shakes
As I go by. "Veloum!"

You can tell which house is the chief's said Will
There is the chief knocking down a mango from his tree
Before becoming Protestant he wore the antelope mask
To the puberty ceremonies, a screaming and a thumping hid the ground.

The elephants came
They were easily overpowered
The dogs came
And barked. The more fertile parts of the ground area flowered.
It was dark. Zaire
Means River. Mobutu
Is King. This means nothing
To the grass. But to the people who pass
This way, it means something. Hip bone

Thigh bone and chest bone, it may come to pass,
Pass into subservience under a moon
That shines equally on Paris and on Gaboon.
The hill wears the mask of a traitor. Will
Drives around and then up and down this hill.

Being here
Gave him a sense of his "destiny," I think,
In a way that
Being in Chicago would not—being
In these dried places, with no place ever to go,
To arrive at, to drive to.

The air
Is faded
Has faded
Is fading
Away
From the river
You see
Dissociated houses
Also very rich Belgian rush
Residences but not
As from the other side (Brazza)
Do you have the Congo right there
To walk up to
And the woman in the boat and the grass.

"They appeared on the scene immediately.
I was handcuffed and knocked about.
They carried me away;
I was not even allowed to walk.
From the prison to the truck

They tossed me about like a stick of wood.
I was taken to the airfield
And immediately thrown into an airplane.
They twisted my neck.
I was badly mistreated.
I arrived in Elizabethville
And came out of the airplane
Like a common bandit—"

Independence brought a lot of death with it.
It brought Lumumba with it and threw him away.

"There are no more tribes in the Congo
There are no more Bakongos or Bangalas
There are no more Wagenias
We have only one free people—"
Tshombe, on the other hand,
Refused, even, to let Lumumba's remains
Be sent to his family.

The insects!
The insects of the Congo and of Zaire
Some known, some still being studied, some
Probably still unknown, are terrifying—
Landing, biting, and leaving, like a traveling death zone.

I cannot deem the rough of this hotel!
The speaking into a welled tube at night.
The grouch of linen. Movimento di windows. Outerness
Wearing masks
The mask of a maiden with a pointy chin
And narrowed but widening eyes, a thin
Fragile smile. The elevator

Takes me up instead of down! Il faut
Partir! Valery Larbaud's *Journal
de A.O. Barnabooth*, and, as well,
Henri Michaux's *Ecuador*,
I fling into my bag.

N'Zambo says, I don't carry baggage.
His wife carries the baggage.
I do not carry the baggage. I am no and have no wife.
And I have a bad back. Into the
Cool air, in an orange cotton dress, goes N'Zambo's wife
With one suitcase under her arm
And another in her other hand.

Everybody will read these
Verses in Zaire. Everybody will talk about
The statements they hold dear. But
What about Bird Africa? what about Luck Africa?
Angle Africa? Eat Africa? and Sunk Africa?

N'Zambo has arrived at the airport,
The airport of bella Kinshasa. Here, as the night heaves
And coughs gropingly, fifty-five persons
Are fighting at the same place
To get tickets at a hornets'-nest-like window.

Here, you wait here, says N'Zambo. His wife
Waits here. And I wait here. Jillian
Is standing in the middle of the vast
Airport hall.

Burundi, Upper Volta, Côte d'Ivoire, and Nigeria
Are places you can't go to from here
Because of political conditions, explains N'Zembi.
However, here, look at this ticket. Your
Plane should be coming in any time now—in three or four hours.
To the balcony (airport terrace) we rise
Shined on by the warm night eyes
Of Zairian stars. Jillian has her own "security group,"
A man from the Peace Corps to help her get on the plane.

The Colonials came
With disorientation
With exploitation
With aggression
With contempt
With no caring
With thinking
They were the people
They were the earth
They were the men
And theirs was the space
And the time

And, often, the Africans let them
Drooping in the sun
Not knowing what
They were up to

And by Colonial standards
The Africans were terrible
By African standards
The Europeans, as magic, existed.

44

But the Blacks weren't part of a magic world
For the oil-spattered-pants-scattered Belgians,
Germans, French (and English). They were "gooks,"
They were part of a White nightmare, they could be put to use.

Meanwhile these Europeans
Educated some Africans
Built up cities
Brought them a language
And a universal religion—
No more thunder in the cheekbones
No more crocodile knees.

Proferring, too,
A cash-crop economy
They fucked-up the old village-
Self-sufficiency economy, ploughed
Young men into the cities
And, finally, granted Independence

After the other life was almost gone—
The tribe, three wives, old man,
Manioc, dancing in the straw, saying
Gandara saloum to make the crops grow—
Almost, but not completely—

Civil courts still hand down convictions
For witchcraft. Leaders do monstrous
Things, unable to rule if they're not devils.
Christianity affects the lives, as
Do politics, and the city, but it is
Hard to tell where anything really is
Or where it is going.

One thing Africa has, it's plenty
Of that kind of thing! is help,

Extremely interested help from every Left and Right party
Of the European, Asian, and American world,
Each of them wanting its minerals, its land, and its support,
Its "voice" in U.N. assemblies
Before the final war—
Those four over there, in blue
Suits, heading for the Cosmos—ce sont les russes!

Nel servizio diplomatico
Esiste una categoria
Chiamata "hardship." You get extra dollars
Hundreds of thousands of additional Zaires
For living and working in Kinshasa
Or other Zairian cities or its bush.

"What you get is the naked, raw thing in Africa—
Life without sheets, or blankets. You see it in the market
In Kinshasa, where everything is cheap.
People are lying around and walking around. They are
Squatting and begging around. (We sleep in the street.
Under us, the street sleeps.) In the village each family has a hut.
This city is their one big hut. And the city is the scene
Of behavior of the kind you find in village and hut." Jillian comes to my
    hotel
Because she doesn't have any place to stay. She
Opens the window and won't close
The shutters. A hot, wet
Heat shine comes in. What
Happened to her Black boyfriend? "He was at the University,"
She says, "and, well, Mobutu closed it down
And sent all the students back to their villages—he is
Hundreds of miles in the bush now, no way to come back
To Kinshasa, and to me. . . . Well,
The part I really like, I lived

On this courtyard, it was actually a sort of market,
Everybody always talking,
And always lying around—African, really African," she said.

We didn't bring our wives because they weren't invited,
Confided N'Jombe. And, besides, we poets don't
Marry literary girls. Those girls, they are other
Ones, who like the writings. We prefer
A woman who takes care of the home, at least those
Are the ones we have married—not the literary
Roses who come serving me the dangerous prose of
Food and drink at the Zairian Club des
Écrivains, girls, not married, and in the
City, and doing all right—calm, like
Everyone else, in an ambiance, all the same, of physical excitement.

5. KENYA. SAVANNA

In the great, bracing air of Kenya
The lion runs. Seeing a lion
And two lionesses together,
The Italian woman said,
"È il leone,
La sua moglie, e la sua madre"—
Id est, the wife's mother,
A sort of chaperone
To the lion and to his wife.

The lion's muscles
Are amazing. The air
Is filled with lions' grace.
Viewed without any
Human component around,
The lion is sensational
Simply of and in himself.

Luciano on the other hand,
Returned from a "Montale Conference,"
The first one, celebrating
The first anniversary of Montale's death,
Says he is "exhausted,"
Says it in Italian
And turning, neither
Like a lion nor a roebuck
Nor any other of the lion's prey,
Those ones who are always
On tiptoe sniffing for the lion,
Into the elevator goes, in America, up to his apartment.

Power in the forefoot and power in the back
The sleek musculature doubling up all over,

Or seeming to, before leaping to attack—
I spent ten dollars on a book
That would have cost two dollars anyplace else
Just to have something to read—anything—
About the lions. A lion is sleeping.
Another lion, a lioness, a "girl," is almost sleeping at his side.

Being depressed is middle class
Said Cornelia's mother
But this is not enough.
The lion is not depressed, it's true,
But neither does he have a social class.
The lion is not upper class
He is dirty
He lets things fall all over him
He is uncouth
He lies around with the lioness asleep all day.

Yes, you left me to run around
Without you and by myself.
At least you didn't leave me out there
On the savanna, subject to the appetites of the lions!

The lion stands up
With a great deal of assurance.
He is not a romantic sort.
The lioness is there and he is there.
Together, they form smaller lion animals.
These run, jump, play, and attack.
Any one of them could give me, if I saw him
Alone, a heart attack.

The lion is admirable
In one way
But in another
He just fills up his stomach
And then sleeps
Until he's hungry again
Then does the same.
Doing this, he
Is powerful.
People
Who live this way
Become fat—and uninteresting.
The lion, however, knows
When he is hungry.
When he is old
It is hard for him to hunt.
The lion becomes mangy
And weak.
Sometimes, just for a second,
His old grandeur shows through—
He evokes the fear of death
In some young giraffe, or antelope,
Or wildebeeste, at the close of day.

The Anglo-Saxon poet characteristically
Presents himself as a good lover, wrote Arthur Waley;
The Chinese poet, as a good friend. The African poet
Often writes poems to his mother (sometimes the mother is Africa).
He presents himself not as a son
Who is there, to work, and to help to keep away the lions,
But as a son who, gone far away, still thinks with passion
Of the warmth and other attractions of his first home.

Is the lion awake? What
Roaring Americans
At the windows of my motel! No,
It's not the Americans.
It's not a lion either. It's
Some elephants
Making a ferocious racket breaking all
The limbs (both live and dead branches) from the trees.

In the Maasai village,
Flies, attacking
Nose, mouth, eyes
You can hardly see
Much less breathe
The Maasai's air.

Maasai drink
Steers' blood from a leather-and-bone vessel,
A kind of long, thin cup that is being held out to me
Next to a thousands-of-flies-thick hut
In their cattle-compound home.

The young woman pilot (English)
Says, when I ask about Maasai
Religion (we are passing
Over "agglomerations of their huts"),
"They don't have any!" Amazing!
"They're simply savages!" And on she flies.
Later she confides to me,
"This place was beautiful once,
Before Independence!" The Maasai, meanwhile,

Do nothing that's not determined by religion.
If you eat a wild animal, the lions will kill your cows.

I read, in
An essay by Kenyatta,
About the Gikuyu—
They would apparently look right through you
If you talked about being sonless in that tribe.
You have to have a son, for, without one,
You never can come back, after death,
To what is best in life: being alive,
Or knowing you are, or feeling you are alive
In the warmth and in the bosom of the clan.

Lighting fires for you
A son!
A son's son, a son's son's son—
He brings you back in.

Twins have to be killed.
This is wasteful
And cruel, but of
Each two one is a demon
And both must be killed.

I feel so far away from this,
As far away as I do from the life of the zebra—
I feel far from Luciano, too, and the Montale Conference,
From the Zion of Ancient Rome, and from the village under the ground of
    the ancestors.

However, this idea of ancestors
Is quite prevalent.

Anyone who dies, or whom you kill,
Immediately becomes an ancestor.

When a wife becomes a mother
Her husband takes another wife
To make love to him and work for him. The other
Gives all her time to the child.

Polygamy, a crime
In many countries, thought of
As a good time in others,
Is a practical matter here—

No lost or unfortunate women
In the village. No prostitutes.
Your brother dies, you marry your brother's wife.
Everyone is taken care of, and connected
To each other, and to the ancestors
In the village under the ground.

The stones
Didn't move
When the birds
Flew so fast
You would think
It would move
Even the stones
Suddenly leaving
Red, violet
And almost totally
Not plain.

The elephant lifts
The big sheet

Of plastic stuck to his trunk
And tries smashing it
Against the ground. He
Stamps it with his left foot,
Raises it and stamps on it again
And again, slowly, for a long time
On the hot, gray-green savanna.

The drive empty for two hours!
We had to get up at
Five and a quarter hours
To see Kilimanjaro
Covered by mist
And now no animals
A zebra gives two nickels a
Lion eighteen the rhi-
Noceros is the jackpot!
Then we see the rhino
Mother and her child
Bathing (?) (eating? drinking?)
In a little pool
One-fifth cool kilometer in the distance
She is dangerous says N'Gambo
Think, then some
Time later say I, Let's
Get out of here! The Kil-
Imanjaro now has
The sun. Well,
It's a great sight, I suppose
(A bit boxed after the rhinoceros),
Seeing the snow
Way up high, when
It's so infernally hot down here.

The vultures and the jackals
Approach the carcass
In a kind of ecstasy (mixed
With fear) of eating and
Approaching and backing up and eating and
Approaching and getting and backing,
Or flying, a little bit, up, and
Eating and then coming back down.

The hippopotamuses don't like the climate,
Everyone said.
And that's why they spend all day in the river.
I thought this was stupid and bound to be wrong
But apparently it isn't. Either the climate
Of East Africa changed, or they migrated. Probably
They migrated. But why did they come?
What ghastly necessity obliged hippo
To run in great masses, against their
Common interests, away from a climate they
Loved, to the scaling, baking dryness of a horrible (for them)
Area and then resign themselves
(Intelligently?) to rivers? Who was the hippo who led them
Away from the danger? And what leader found them the rivers?
Or were they led by many? Did some, not finding rivers, die?
At night they go up on the banks and feed on the grass.

In the hotel there are civilization conditions.
A hundred yards outside it, nothing obeys anyone.

As attractive as a wild condition is, I just don't have the teeth
Or the paws with claws or the power in my back and legs to do it.

I didn't even when I was young. I'd have lasted,
Perhaps, five or six minutes—
If I were lucky a few days, a few
Hours. Impossible!

Of course I wouldn't have been surrounded
By (near me) two hundred or so
Members of my tribe (species), each one
Alert, on the tip of his toes, his tail
(Or her tail) swishing, head, even when browsing,
Turned slightly aside
To sniff out, or spot, the presence of a lion,
The burny, unmistakable smell, some top flicker of the grass.

I thought so, looking at the zebras
For a while.
Zebras are young and strong
And race, with style.
They are styled in black and white, zebras.
Their ambition is not to be eaten
By the lion or the cheetah.
As they move about, you see them gazing to the side
And ahead and back, as they lawn-mow and,
Toward evening, seem to glow, and they grow
And multiply in the wild savanna.

"The hippopotamuses
Are all Communists,"
I wrote when I got to bed,
Extremely tired, exhausted,
Thinking of
The way they looked at me
With suspicion, perhaps

Even a glint of hostility
Just eyes and nose above the stream.

The tsetse flies
Are unsung heroes of Africa.
Over enormous areas
They dominate everything.
Elephants, Maasai, lions, flamingos, everyone, everything
Runs away from them. They carry
Sleeping sickness surprise.

I am glad I wasn't turned into an ancestor,
While strolling aimlessly around on the Serengetti,
By the bite of a tsetse fly.

The shots! the shots! are nothing
Compared to one tiny tswish of a tsetse fly.

With a subtle change of the light—it's not so subtle!
It is night on the savanna, and those animals are in trouble
That the lion hunts.
Then dawn comes, with a slighting wave
Of a hand of wisp of smoke and cloud, the bones stay
There but the flesh is gone, to be part
Of other flesh. The lion goes lightsome now
Whether waking or sleeping, thanks to his eating.

The Rift is a huge dominatingness of non-presence
Dividing, which will cut you one half
Of Kenya and make you another. It is a rift
Dividing Maasai from other Maasai. It makes
A difference in the climate. Geology looks at it

With scholarly and mercenary eye. The dawn goes to sleep in it.
Here, you can tell what Africa was like
Hundreds of thousands of years ago, geologically.

Now rain blow, storm lines, Rift-caused, then showering
Sunlight past accolades of drift.

Returned from the Maasai Mara
The lions and the savanna, and back
From Amboseli, as well,
Kilimanjaro and its rhinoceros
And last night
In Nairobi with its guns
In the hands of soldiers
I sit at the hotel (Serena) and drink coffee
At the yellow wedge of this table by
The purple wedge of this pool, while a hedge
Of tourists passing through
Are dividing themselves up into a car.

At Maasai Mara
There were buffalo first, then
A jackal, a carcass,
And a vulture—then a lion
And then impala, wary of the lion.

Elephant mothers do not decree
The lion to be present chiefly
Because for lions an elephant baby (a calf)
Is a manageable thing to kill and eat.
Not so a big elephant. With big elephants around
Like swinging, wavy, shipwrecked, cargoed scenes
In a friendship series, calf is safe and sound
Protected from the lion in the thwack and whack and bumping of the trees.

One of which (elephants) nearly killed us,
A female, charging for our "bus"
Whereupon Julius vavoomed us fifteen more feet away
Toward some other pious-looking elephants at the bay
Of some serpentine now falling-apart trees. Hey
Julius I said what if she had gotten us, knocked
Over the bus. Oh said he, then we just
Raff as heard as we con. And at our laughter
(Mine, Julius's, that of one French couple, three Japanese
And Margaret of Australia whose camera caused the scene)
The heavy, tusked, wide-eyed symbiotic elephant would back away
Justly terrified. What? Laugh? No,
Julius said, *Raff, rafv* the engine!

Later, the next night,
Margaret is deemed a danger
To the UNESCO conferees
Invisibly (i.e. unknown to me) being
In the Serena for several days.

No—hand on my shoulder—no
Dat—grapefruit juice, with
Ice—No dat
Lady in dis hotel. Where
Go you, sir? And gently are we expunged

Into the Kenyan night. You go
Find dis everyplace Nairobi
Tonight, says the
Taxicab driver
Whose back is becoming visible at the lights.

The animal scene
Is a scene and a set, a
Theatre inside a country. Kenya
Profits from it, lives
By it, but isn't it. Banded men in Nairobi
And standard men in Nairobi and granted women
And an estaminet of money white and green
Set off another, central human scene. And then
In the middle, there is Julius, for
Example, whose grandfather was a hunter, he
(Julius) is a Protestant, with just
One wife, enjoying the benefits
Of *something*—comparatively Kenya
Is "doing all right." La Côte d'Ivoire, says everyone,
Is prosperous as well.

When the Rift came down through Africa
From Egypt to Kenya and Uganda,
It did not fill with water
And become a Congo—there was nothing,
No boat, anything, before airplanes,
That could cross it, but, by that time, everyone
Was used to being on one side
Or the other, and not to crossing over.

Don't go to Mombasa. It
Is remplie with German tourists
And they romp the beach. Just a swimming hole
For Tedeschi, said the brown-olive-fair Italian
Woman I'd have given anything for of to have had the house
Keys. The lips of her turned bronze as she turned away
And I didn't see the promontory of the bird saints, either,

Or the woman's keys, nor the oily fair rumps of Mombasa
The City by the Sea, Kenya's industrial mermaid domino.

Termites in Kenya
Have big, really tremendous
Houses of their own. Termite control
Would mean destroying both termites and house.

In downtown Nairobi
Modern it is and dark. I take a path
(Turn) onto the Avenue Moi
Formerly Avenue Kenyatta—
One kilometer further
And I'm home—
The Hotel Serena. It is
(Its lot is) littered with cabs.

ON THE EDGE

Sleeping one day beside the Zuyder Zee
Dan was awakened by a noise of honks—
A situation quite unknown to me:
I spent my childhood in a sort of Bronx—
I placed a goldfish bowl upon my knee—
Angelica was packed inside my trunks.
At Harvard I wrote home "I'm coming back!"
And did, and through the country like a crack

The train sped home. Dan took a blossom down
From off the blossoming tree. I slept all night
Then spent the next day walking through the town.
Angelica woke up to Roland, light
And bright and fair. Dan sighed and looked around.
He couldn't see Roberta anywhere.

As in—Crete, near the ditch—old grave spot (gray spot) as
By the Greece's Acropolis's invisible waters—Parthenon—
Agh, what vents!—and you too, monopolistic
Bypath-or-street-ways, little Merkaton
Of old Athens plus light blue shimmers from the cliffs
In other places and I couldn't explain
What I felt at Heraklion, I'm sorry, or with
My nose pressed to the train—everything else stubbing
And stumping. I'd planned—but wanted to know. Reading,
In the day, complaining, stormed, red and blue lights
Until traffic, I think, is right here in the chains
Of what's holding all these chairs, this
Stuff together—up in the air, I think.
Zett calls, and now I have a drink.
Cold is the kitchen sink.

Forms to feel it out
Quietness to bring it in
As someone "felt friendly" Stendhal pushed the door
Egg was inside, the Easter Egg of Monsieur Montelfior

Who made the wind his messenger
Outside, in the penniless air
Of the warm white sidewalk and the street, thinking
Whether I am in the cloth with her or not
Then suddenly to think

Finger in the beehive
Harry says Watch out!
A drove of French novels
Particularity of stone-dead windowpane, without charity
Or trump—esthetico indeed! why, I'll
And so you—one minute—are falling, it is orchids

Paris, C's apartment
Claudio on the phone, the receiver
Tucked between his chin and his shoulder

A panther has escaped
From Nankra's Zoo! I lay confidently
Embedded in the light green grass of the Bosco
While A. A. de Celestin smoothed out her thanks
Blouse sleeping softly and mandarinly toward me
No sensations but in commands, you too
Storm and confusion. Roberta? Angling—whom?

She lifts a shoe. Where is the other one?
Jean-Claude came to dinner, etc. Sitting here, it's a café

Summery Sunday, Notre Dame des Champs,
Noël and Joanne come to take us both
Out riding to the forest. You have *gants*,
Being *frileuse* as I am not. We wear coats
Because it's, after all, the winter *temps*
And no one's in the Bois in little boats.
Ecstasis perigrensis. Première acte.
Mutas mutanda. Life in love lungs locked.

The scene is—writing—but remembering the buffering strums
Memories of a de-cupola'd Hotel de Fleurus
Triggered with leaves sidewalks a fluttering
I say something as red clouds and you said
I remember the name—going forward

Now I want to. Forces! yelled Jim Dine, and
Fairfield Porter, surprised, "Maybe! Let's just go and see."
These extreme persons of the time
And the forward and back—
To café! a cold university

Thanks for your criticism
I am thinking
Feeling my way across the yard
B-Zunk doesn't write me I figure she's
Having a love affair with Arc
Having had not much going but making love to each other
Our relationship soon fell apart

Dan is a hero of a different nature
The Colossus of America, England, and France
He is of an ordinary stature
Remarks someone at a dance
Dan dances with her and then he goes away.

The mountain of roses and the dog. What is that ripple?
Happiness, a street vine, and the nude
Weather forecaster, now dressed and out, it's day
For this monument, as if life
Depended on it, lilac, that scent, so many times!

The water fills with flowers—hibiscus, waterlilies. Ventur-
Ing then when Jan and I got in the boat
My parents objected, Haven't you got to the wrong hot spot
Of water if what you're really going after is adventure?

Adventure of the third kind
Desire driven from the mind
To the Greek statue arm muscle
We floated and then
Five years later it's of a doctoral order
Board walls of a house
And flowers tacked onto it. Hey, shining.
And Bart said You're not a scholar but a jeweler
And Schlumberger said Keep talking—until guns fired.
She hangs the wash on hooks, outside.

"What's the matter, anyway?" I say
To my friend
Toujours plus pessimiste
A quality I find assez adorable
I thought if he could just
Now we are racing toward the dust
Quality of a friend with the trace of a suit on it
Blue-brown, a necktie, red, yellow, compromising
Avec ze style of ze time, so Wallace Stevens said
"You should keep the same style," this little guy
Said A. W. jokingly, partly, has done more
For the philosophy of—Jesus! If we had time—The green ledge
Walking sideways on it without
But full of, interest, by being purely
Physical, Leger, at the age of thirty-three, a finite hem
Explaining things to me
As another always interpreted. I don't,
I said snobbishly, like it much, but

Well, you know, and everything
He liked Spring, the sweet spring
Then backing down the water (alley) with a blot
With friendship talked a lot
And was indifferent
However, there he is!

And other Elizabethan literature
I said: It's great!

Oh, it's great
                all right,
                        said he
But would you read this? I'm so
Depressed!
                What?
                        We—after death
And his passing—but
                        also ours

Reading what I was reading, like the girth
Of that building—from the *Four Quartets*
To the *Macchu Picchu* of Neruda, neither
There nor in between was there to answer
The inevitable brio of light
Not surreal, not fragmentary or anything but
A white sidewalk—do you think?

If I had known then, in nineteen-fifty . . .
There was one introductory class at the university
And others at various places and times. The *u* was difficult.
The noses of cars kept dodging on the street
With knowledgeable humans inside them—
Not simply having experiences and growing up
And trying to judge the various stages of joy
And ecstasy and how do I get published? but
Actually participating in the crescent
And crossed edge of Being—I thought.
Sometimes, eating with you, I'd drop my plate
Or glass. You said, They are infinite. However
Just this morning I see the old man, presumably a worker
With shellfish, I don't know!
What I did the chairs were bunched

In each café. "Get out of the way." Ovvero, climb with me, the play *Truck*
Is being presented. So many girls then
Sidewalk hitting with its cement
The fabulous others who gradually fade into myself
Like the Epidaurus Theatre, starring Acts One and Three—
Act Two is your own revolution.

To deal with frost-bites
Into the old earth, on the surface of which all
Societies lived: French bourgeois society
Bon soir, Tante Adélie, ed entra la cugina Karamazov
On the edge
Of the cup,
Of the street,
Of reading Mallarmé
The door opens on the same spaces again.
Bird news was strafing past the window
Full feather time. I opened it and went out
Into the car.

And then last night (198?) the A.M. air was sharp
Outside the bar, Place de la Contrescarpe
And I walked home alone, not wishing to
Get in the car, since Hugues was drunk. I thought
Being alone quite the best thing to do—
And with my small red guidebook's help I brought
Myself to where I lived, cette jolie rue.

Our modern—fragmentary—Dan stands up—it's about time—reason
Sunrise—he is going to start
White sleeves
But day puts its finger in his eye
Eyes. The white vagary temple is starting up
Aislewards—
The waves were coming home! against a tree
They wash. Fifteen

Years it lasts, and no end in sight, and no
Beginning. A topic is pink white pink stripes.
Drunk. On gin, lemonade, and fizz
White as the cover of the book and of the pages inside.
Fifteen years, or is it ten or twenty that it lasts. Sexual forces,
Greek logic, Aphrodite, in statue form, born Irish girls, smiling
And removing a blouse, beginning
To snow in here, writing out notes
And flying down the street, noble as far as
Bed could be commanded by what's outside.

Or he was writing, sitting amidst the unpacked trunks
In a state of composition, while the trunks, then, are in a state of
Saturday afternoon position, as at the Mayor's house

What she was then—what a beautiful bloom!
And people sitting round their desk for hour
After hour could only exclaim, "Well, fine, boom, to hell with it,
Let's go to Tahiti, anywhere,
Out of this worm-eaten building!" At last
You wonder about the filtering down of consciousness
Till even the moth, so sensitive to light,
Is stepped on, on the stairs. The band plays
Full out—

Sometimes the feeling was so strong it came out
Sometimes was dancing or "rage" (being mad)
Biting and sleeping and then in the beautiful morn-
Ing, when to be young was very heaven,
The yellows, light on buildings' separate heaven
Of warm apartments, not too warm, now, open
A light-bulb light—
The limping man and the doctor—complements
The drink and the thirsty girl—oxygen

In questo momento scrivevo poesie
Al soggetto di un grande industriale

The subject is not in the world—the subject's
A limitation of the world. Thus, no true subject.
The Hotel de Fleurus was of the world
Now vanished, literally said Bob
It's turned into a private house, of many apartments
No more the door unopenable from inside
It wasn't a "subject" however. The nature
Of hotels is a subject—whose thigh?

Red bird, white bird, jumping around the house. "When you're not
Inspired, when you feel 'dry' just write anything!" False
Scholarship, false Solomon's Seal
Am I the height of Heaven or is blue the thrust
Of some addlepating ecstasy that's flooding me? Cancel
Your bills, believe in me. Proud to be Representative
Of Frock-White-Flowering Day appeared on doorstep
With Russian Moods and Count Weight. If only someone had told me,
Some intelligent man, said Stendhal,
To write two hours every day, whether
"Inspired" or not, I would have saved ten years of my life.

Sitting in a tiny café I read Mallarmé's *Le Livre*
I don't know whether or not this is something I want
I wasn't happy but I was absorbed and I was curious
I felt on the brink of something,
I kept reading, and in the book there was nothing doing
It may have been all just a laundry list but something was taking place in
    me
Did I have a mistress? Maybe. Had we been to bed? Well, not quite.

Thursday, three in the afternoon. Learning
Dutch. . . . Five minutes
Sandwiches . . . the fury in the hall ninety-nine francs
Don't like Like it Madame
Dantonville return four chemises front

Window alive serenities festive
Remember call BO 6-2279 Magyars
A visit in the sea . . . cruet . . . vast availability . . . five sleds—shirts
And then a tremendous space
Then space   space   space
Following: a list
Of debts?

Tears to remember again
One fourth or one sixth part of it

So I went dancing out into those streets
But on knees and on my knees it was the day
Lying catalyzed, a book. I'm not a roof if also if you mean that!

He actually made a mistake said John. It's wrong.
"Gyrene" but we continued. But Mallarmé
Fippery ovoid subject but I didn't pay
Attention. Loaf. Lilac book.

Martin McScrumbold who controlled the sedge
For fifteen companies of marble fusions
Clambered aboard the high financial towers
To make himself the toast of sanctity,
Seeming to be more holy than he was
By manufacturing gimmicks propped galore
Against the definite walls which adversaries
Totalled between themselves and him in vain.
Sunday he smashed the sleep. . . .

Summer on the folding step
And somewhere on the other.
A side step. Sunlight. Perhaps it would phone me
To be so ablution inseparable
Twenty-five years
Before nineteen-eighty. And bright

Flocks of automobiles go past
Green flight
Of centimeters, one, and up and down.
In the morning to look for
Blisters in the sidewalk Egypt of Their Time

The Journal of I forget
Virgil's Eclogues how they connect to the life
The show-business falseness is carrying on.
The bed is stored over where the light
Was, with futile and inconsistent flight. O "scatalogue" that gives me
Rushing around from feuding hours of the night
To spirited activation of the doll
Speaking in the morning
Huge halls. Not nearly buffered very long.

An ideal book for me was also that
I wanted to have and give up every subject
And I suspected it would end in about two seconds
So many painters were cracking their plates in the seminary
Of other persons' kindness while a large snowflake,
Faintly and intolerably slowly, falls. Flirting and courting heartbreak.
The Greeks—A brick blockade
Is knocked down. If I'm to be a painter, help me with your tears!
He said. Then I sat down.
Is it this—a historical
Meaning—out of your control
I crossed the wave
Of pink cement
Dawn! and study not far away!
With Eleanor, containing the football
Its footfalls, its stories of cinema'd scorn.

Bear—
Alone I think
It's

A laundry list
But still happy

Here are a few phone numbers, too

Ulla said Don't came to visit me in Sveden
Badly I threw myself as if from out of a
Bucket onto the train. Hallo goodbye said she
My boyfriend is here. I will not see you. But her flat face
In Paris, with the light hair in her eyes, her capacious
Be-loving-me sexitude, hunh, what's happened
To that? The Stockholm railway station loomed
With mounds of produce in a bag
Of each it held

Writing
Saving ten years

A blouse (blue)
Came in the entryway, drama
To perception
Instantaneously and in light
Of the moving seconds
I'm sitting and talking
Or else, exhausted, glad and sorry
Dog straining forward
Hating the seemingly automatic activity
Either language or either brain does on its their own
Wrong with so much fucking literature
French boredom bong
But as I romp around
Blonde bang bomb
Scowling
Event, climatic, and strong
How if we all came over
Or you come to my place—

Why not throw this, said Jim,
Into the fulminating fireplace? Giggled, savagely aft
While maturity stole a scarf and took her place
Beside Janice who was dreaming of a plan
For a whole season. Stanley: We displace
So many phantoms. Jean: Garage.

The ecstatic muddle does, didn't it, take place
February seventeenth nineteen-fifty Samothrace Tuesday immense

Dan walks around. He waves
His hands above his head.
Upon his tombstone it shall be engraved
He did what no one else could do instead.
He was a morning slasher. He engraved,
Summarily, upon a day of red,
The melancholy taxi of a kiss
Upon a sidewalk edge, for emphasis.

We walk out
And at a desk
On a bridge
Popular leafy upstairs
A form oh to go
Pink and white
Rose "oceanness"

I'm sympathetic to animals and all that, said.
Rescuing the fly flew into
Above water splat. Sit looking at
Specific gravity on its wings.

Crossing my sleeves with hers
Nineteen-fifty
Prepare
The quilts, mattress, bed-covers

Circa nineteen-fifty-four
Larry says Why don't you stay there
Another bluish bit
Of sidewalk and her hair
Human feather

Window, diamonds flashing
A. hard at work
Extemporaneous fingers
American Claw is reading about Van Gock (Go)
Pages of Keats (*Endymion*) This side of the cluck
Is belted with sunshine, G. Entwery
Also is recommending movie junk
And class ("I don't know why de Mourneville
Doesn't get off his ass and make more films . . .")
All the witty things we know are wasting
That used to be the center of the world.

Harry walks with me through the show of roses.
We talk about Maxine. Elizabeth
Is dancy at my side, as she supposes
I like her. I am somewhat out of breath.
With Jean I walk along and the place closes.
We dance beside the Marne. I love my desk.
As a drowning man to a spar I hold on to my desk (F. Kafka)
Hydrangeas bloom, seen from beyond the desk (Flutsworth)

And friends call Janice sits on the bed Frank calls
The momentary euphoria of understanding
Dan, much preoccupied, steps to the landing
Doesn't free me from these feelings after all
After all she was like a bird, flown off
Seems more than I could do when I mistook
Shadowing for boxing, evening for no lights in the hall
But now a fine mercurochrome like the dog's complacent ball
Into these fire vicinities. Frank said it was like it al-

Ways was, except that we were broaching entire infinities
This time, and, if I drink any more coffee I'm going to ride
Into the sky! Janice at nine in the city, cold are celebrities.
The fire plugs are cold. While they are alive
The whistle is metal, was not foot—needing—awfully—years before.

Avenue du Maine, with that wall with the posters on it
Everywhere saying it's forbidden to have posters on it,
Where I lived in the time I was a drink student
And a clink student of all flourishing Proust-things and I went out
Into the fulminating gravel of that damp sleep. That never came out
How civilized you are! we are! I was! It is, cow in and then out.
I went "to bed" with the two Swedish girls, Ana and Svenita, I don't
    remember,
In fact, their names—
You have frightened me into these staminas
Where the different associations they come running!
The bloom of helio-plaster, "medicine of the sun,"
Will absolutely cure your solar system, clean it out
So there'll be summer everywhere and always. Huh?
I loved the following women: BLANK
Out of discretion—But . . .

Alleyed-to-interview maze. I pleaded
Guilty, saying, I'm glad you're that,
Big, thin, notable, heart-
Shaped, sweet, irregular,
Smiling, quiet, tanned,
Around. Whereupon a ticket machine goes thumping
"Air raid! O climbing ceilings!
Birds that didn't add to visiting things!"

Paris
        And nineteen-fifty-two
    Fresh air

Clean warm spring morning
And I am in love with you
            Answers!
There were more answers than there were questions
Almost—questions I had to make up—

What is a "stair person"?
Do you know what a "bid minor" means?
Do scows have ears?
How many charge accounts can fit into a building?
And so, in love with you,
I walk the streets
Pretty littered asphalt, hut to roots,
Walking, talking

One shoe
Is that October or is that March
Summery day
God says, "Don't take that drink!"
What portion is two? what sidewalk?

Accidentally
Running into her. The wave
(One second). Hello. Admired Miranda!
O wild West Wind, thou breath of Autumn's
Being! Getting into Harvard (half a minute).
The log head and the pavement, stone hotel.
Dear K., I am
Leaving (three times). Why, though?

Vanishing into the Nile this comes only once

Dan was waking up,
Finding the world, some fluff from blossoms landing on him
A short breeze ruffling his
Clothes, summering sleeves, a little sun

Greatening in the white to be a big one
And that fresh air so invigorating
That he jumped up
Feeling where he wanted to go
He turns, then, sees

Thousands—need for food—all the critics say
Almost all—leaning on a railing
And looking out far—nails in the shoes—riverbank
And the motory smell
A white horse comes up
In a non-animal civilization—
The established ruins (products of four hundred years)
While the dream of the day
Is in the arms, later
Darling wronged
Sweetheart
I bray
Like a donkey (five seconds)
And the music is then of laughs (one
Second et demie). K. K. finds a cat and feeds it
And its kittens (seven days)
This moment and then coming
Completely up to date (almost), like a bat,
Seeing a cloud and thinking "It's Cleopatra!" Two seconds.
Knowing she'll take off her clothes (instantaneous).
Realizing I can't stay in the apartment
Cold, breezy nights
A collaboration (eight years, though
For the time spent working
Actually about two hours). Percentage of days
Counting the days (one,
Approximately). Times I had to work
Instead of doing what I thought
I wanted to do, some. But times I did work

And didn't do what my "life-boast," "life-bomb," or
"Shoulders-o'-stone" wanted done—
Flowers in every window of the street
Music playing behind. Friends come around. That's an excuse
(One dog). And the times, the times
Asleep, trying to sleep, making love, drunk

I notice the sunrise—it's quite something, the day!
My desire—Eleven A.M. too
And five-thirty, just before dark

Mathilda Roberts bumped against a window
Seeing a sheep, but Dan came through the day
Walking, his white coat hanging over his arm,
Left arm, and what could she (La Roberts) say
"I have been falling asleep," he said,
"In rocky different places. Beside a peak in Gstaad
Once, and by the Ceremonial Summer Beak in Tchad
As well as of course beside the well-tamed
Sea of Zuyder
Jusqu'au plus soif. The wind is very strong!"

Another day guilt is all I'm feeling
The gloves go on and off in simple whiteness
Weather is moving, and personality
Which seems just over the horizon, Greek, and homeless
I walked around
To the back of the car—sunflowers—an April evening
Living (a while) but not living very long. Totals
Of time spent merely in the society
Of other people without improving anything
Learning anything or really
Doing anything (enormous). Time
Music was of the essence (unknown).

A leg moves
To another section of the bed
I am up
Newsily bemused and musing
On what has just happened instead
Of carrying on with it. Proust wrote the book and he was dead
On the bed table, evidence! that suddenly they become
Business men and business women
As the delicate white gloves of the sun
(So dixit Svana)
I got to get up. The gun
Of a new day is pounding got to get
On my jacket's got to get
New translating job jobs at the embassy go to
Get ready for bar tonight, get
Going, up—everything

Bathing and raving—
Classic symphony, outdoor beers. Blue awning. Capes. Stone. The flashing
    substance
Of sleeves and neck and collar and the subtle
Shade of pink in cheek and slight resistance
And then surrender! Lipstick in the puddle
At the umbrella'd table close to Customs!
I—I—you—skirt—it's my—flags—in battle—
Your—by—sleeves—listen—I'm—wait—sperm—ova—
Interest—bud—easy—luck—Vita Nuova—

Never again that Sunday in the Peugeot
Spinning to Fontainebleau! I take a hairpin
And bend it sharply till it is a bow
For a minute it seemed to be there
Small white flag
Of hard dress unburdened
As the poets say
By "time" whose neck

A sheep, buttons
Of a capacious (big, roomy)
Wedge, and then

Used at breakfast to sashay me until
Sitting, somewhat sprawled, in a chair
Reading Lautréamont. Oh for God's sake
Let's group out of here. Lieutenant,
Cross over the glass porcelain men!
Wake up said Janice dear. I was walking
In nineteen-seventy-two, when suddenly
E. L. was nineteen years old, A. R. was twenty-three
And I was almost fifty, cinquante ans—

Now it is later I have just come back
From Africa, to which for the excitement
I went, and Noel still is on his track
Of pneumonology. His wedding statement
However's changed, and Z is gone, a fact
Suggesting their first choice as not the right one.
Both middle-aged and changed by that fantastic
Chimie du temps in almost every aspect

Split seconds of a chair in a café
Time the note on a glass window
Says they are coming Change
To sarabande attire, ice of the Sixties
When to be Decemberish was the soul of claim
To interest and enticement of the muse of flame,
Forties of the gnarled How-to, Fifties of consentment
To split and tower and ropes weather, islands of the
Damned insane Eighties hues cupped in flame
And no car because the secret to get out of, caught in history's game
Scattered about like furniture, too wise to be the main
Movers of things, already too dead?

Reading "Yellow violet"

Appointment with nnn hayerdresser, she says. We are to meet (met)
Later, I don't like to eavesdrop. Soap.

What pompous! what ruckus! and what creates!
The whole women of Proust! the pavannes and the flowing carriages!
The doctors on horseback, their patients behind them in stalls
In Middle Ages weeping, "Cure us, or give us our money back!"
I run and put on my ducking—
Why am I wearing ducking to this place? Whose mirror is that above the
    piano?
It is Ferdinand de Lesseps' or Fernand Léger's! Qu'en sais-je? I may not
    have Stendhal's talent, after all,
To get down what actually took place.

The adornments of these clavicles, says Rodeson
(Panoscopic visions in a multifactored box)
Presuppose an Aegean civilization. You're right! What? I love! (Mayakovsky)

Do you suppose? he said. Oh, I don't know, I—
Well, that's a thought! I'd better use the tele-
Phone! The sails seemed white forever.
It clatters down the stairs. You have a fever
But stand and walk around.

Elizabeth is glad—it isn't raining
Or snowing, but the sun's out. She has just
Become nineteen. She notices
A plan, coming off the wall. That's a MAP,
Old Chinese restaurant, with a small
Waist, back-breaking task,
While sunshine rolls around

Take me with you. You don't love me. Scowl
Blank. Go.

84

"The secret," Harry said, "is that eternal
Fluctuations make us workers here
On this great hill of art, where on a clear
And not-too populous day one notes the vernal
Intemperance of carnival—we cheer
The musing flowers on their slapping way."

And Bukaku hadn't yet met him so had not yet intro-
Duced me to him I was reading, voraciously, Guido Gozzano

The pink air was guzzly a little and fashionable

Harry, in any case, now in appearance, says
"Call up!" The eternity of messengers was behind us
Scattered all over, the roses of the Bois de Boulogne.
It's very convenient to be there, the earth is a phone
So, Worm, you can call anyone—Whose are the fragrant cashews of this
    spring
Of Roman-Indian fragrance, out into that "cool gray dock"—of "advance"

"If only we had done something, really,
Like inventing the steam
Engine. When we do (invent something), though, it instantly dwarfs us."
I thought Rilke must be standing in that zoo,
Said Dan, so I went up to him, I
Thought, but it was von Spitz, inventor of the atomic stream.

A fiery bracelet. Dishes pile up later.
Don't criticize me so much
I couldn't—I will—I don't think anyone will
Remember my sensations. Sometimes it seemed
All I was doing was going to sleep
Or trying not to. Did the smokestack throw
Less fire because of hell me?
In any Etruscan I found it was all there.

If they're not actual—I mean, outside!
I don't care—or think they could be outside,
They are, I can get to them! I plan to speak
To someone—the first breasts of the sky—shush!—Go to sleep!

The house on Hydra when we lived there once
Was a small house whose whiteness was its wall.
We actually stayed there just two months
Of wide, hot summer scrambling into fall.
The waves against the stones made noise like punts
While walk along and Katherine says Good-ball
Good-bye. Goats as from a frieze
Make blunt the room.

So did my white shirt-cuffs—cow path,
Jessica stays at loops, Mycene December
And French autumn, Christmas, blackness, risky
Flower arrangements, so that above the prow
Emeritus mummies appear, clement to wake us up—
The elegant white-pink of an eggshell dusked
By damask in the magician's petrified cloth—

On the side of the sparkling
Glass sliver—something—peace
In its light-red-blue reflection.
Dan puts it to some use

This earliestness has wings, like Fra Angelicos, in cars

The bed was white
Its sheets were
The moon (or what- who-ever was there) was waiting
In the morning
I bent, leaning
From one to another place

Vision of Machu Picchu, God what heights! (one minute)
Botticelli's Venus—two seconds—
Three minutes, eight minutes,
Planning to go there, being there, che splendida giovane!

Do you remember the storms, the depressions, the unbelievable
Disasters? and when you think of them, can you sleep
And eat? I thought my life was going to be a scrapbook,
It turned out, instead, to be a heap.
A heap of what? Noël said, laughing. Joanne was laughing,
Her skirt was on a spot
Slightly blue-colored on her right leg, white skirt
Now her gray eyes peer at Speed across the table top
Speed! tell me, when are you seeing Dan?
As in a Yeats triptych cognitized in a dream
Skittering, warm summer morning. A day of the orange
Expense account of fragile invested sunlight
But I said Which? Orin was switching the lights
I didn't want to think about or forget
The mesh, of the subway, the powder on the table
Is blowing somewhere else.
Irganian Eskimos asked him for his life
In bondage in the snow, to which he savantly replied
Yes and no, sleeping my way out
Focusing on the pale night
Driven into the streets
Desire to find out
Dripping and edged with green and orange paint
What institutions connected to what sensations?
Law to nudity?

Bread without thought.

Advancing to the typewriter (sheep), and unboxedly looking at the sky
    (weak), the
Bones of the climate and the poles, one week

The stems in the throats of those conversations!
The strong young woman emerging—Venus, not
Music playing behind.
At other times, stunned time, time being stunned, stunned
Intervals and times of anxiety's careering like a body
Inside the regular body, with nerves
All that seem in between

In Paris there was no one. It was cold out there
But it was something. Inside you was a baby.
Inside Thomas Hardy was *Jude*. I thought
What is in me? A day of secret stuttering doors is in me

"Elle craque, tu sais, elle absolument craque!" syzygy
And blankets of stars which would put even Dan out on a limb
Of "Unusual groceries!" whereas, touching his chin—Loves, good-bye!
However, my hat doesn't ever get away from them
Keeping so busy I had no time to go out
When anything was open or anybody wanted to go with
Me—You're lucky! said Jim. Do
Come in, said rafafafa of daisies
But necessary be welcome to this town
And sit and read

He is very encouraging, usually, in particular
For whatever you propose. Going to drink coffee
Listen! My head is going to blow off if I do
But yes, let's go, quickly! Aspects of a job
That can only be done magnetically. You've got it!
Laughing and coughing in a brightly lighted street
Or a dull gray one, away from
The bright sun I saw him—the funeral
Men and women glaring at their sleeves unhinged

Do you remember the "real writers" of nineteen-fifty?
Do you remember the pretension of that spot?

Lake Sholem Aleichem was produced off-Broadway in nineteen-fifty-seven—
Dogwoods, meant for the next year, was never done.
Do you remember the bad faggots and the crackpots?
The masses of mouldy customers and the crumps? the grumps
The unsatisfied? Do you recall the Eliot Divide?
The bad, sad, and second-rate, our souls unsatisfied?
Painters shifting a place there with the paintbrush
Ain't doin nothin, nothin that counts! And it
Was true, too—
Apartment-wall-side proposed to a flame
And kept the villains inside
Who wanted to come veering out (melodies) while
Cracking a whip above the dances (waltzes) and
Wouldn't let the moon inside
The paintings! Outside on the side-
Walk side, where time was the clout of all their canvasses,
Men walk by. Sighs
Over Garbo and Dietrich, jumping excitement over Coleman
(Ornette)? Do you remember the cordite starring in *Diaspora*? Good, and
    bad!
What dark red afternoon did Otto Luenig
Afford my snobbery vis-à-vis Stefan Wolpe as Frank crushed
Dissension by seeing the bright in everything? It's cold in here

And it was a dawn
In nineteen-fifty-eight, firing pin on the levees.
A flood is coming! Over the hill
Dan kept moving. Reading Stendhal
La Vie de Henri Brulard in nineteen-eighty
I said my goal be that!

The celebrated "inside-outside" feelings
X wrote Y when he was only twenty-one
A cherry tree (sneeze) of precocity
Annual mump
I wonder about the fig tree

On Island Ump—Hydra
Your red silk is freezing
On this sand-of-me-beep-through-the-car day.
Why a car should talk
(Seemingly) and a head
Be blinded (for a moment) I don't know.
Why am I not a tropical man?
If I can look at all these things and not be blinded, what do I think
I think at one moment and at the next moment I don't
I am blinded
Think
I see the plate
I live in this civilization
Dumbbell

All the same, though, this sad night seemed lost
And others right then, too
Nonetheless blathering hoop-la absconding frequently
Filled my days and creepings with such abundance of regardings
And suddenly (it seemed so) glad fixations on
The non-parliamentary procedures sun
Shining to plate, I said, Dearest when all this is done
When are we going to get anywhere or know anything
Slate, faculty, and pocketbook. Bust, she regarded
The soon-maidened day. Well, we will! she said.

An upward look, which is depenetrated
Southernly, by a stretch of Freud. Oh look at the complexes
The dust road is wet
Clouds' days are climbing all around.

They roll
The top
To show
The lot
How climbed

And clean
The hill was.

But well a day
It stops to say
(The air)
My clouds
Are pillows!

So run, run!
This is not
Herrick nor John Donne
But some modern
Inky fellow's
Prized Armageddon
De syllabes.

And on one opaque filled-with-joy daylight-blue-and-pink-and-white-faced
    morning
She kissed him on the cheek
Whereupon

For five hours of which the first fifty-five
Minutes are the most intense. Joanne, stopping
And with letters

They always do find them, said Dan.
He took the manacles off Schiavona's wrists.
And went home talking about the *Alchemist*
The good the bad acting the dubious kind of direction
The musty smell of the theater and the rest.
D'you like it—them, replied.
This lunchtime. Oh, how—
Bearing secondary (or supernumerary) parts. I am on the ledge
Later the doctored-up paintings and
Alone, cold

Sitting in the bundled coats and thinking Well
It's over. The lamp went out.

The car, quel tas de junk
And U. was at the wheel, ridiculously drunk
And divided between about five girlfriends
I was so much older I should have been in the trunk
But I was there, am, now, however, edging my shoulder
Past C-Jump I could see that with every act
I was hoping and she was singling some quality out
To arrive at later with better but could not afford now
To be the one I buttoned on clothes with; still, there she was
Radiating fullness in the car,
Once home, no chill, relief, cabbage in the dawning
No those are light green cloudlets coming up the trees
So then I go to bed, it's as in the car—snore,
Raffle, awake, then back to slump, and sleep—

The wavy secretary speaks at the bend
Of the desk office, now I am met by the head
Agent. I stand up, the secretary's gone. Good-bye.

Beautiful figure
Of everything! Then
Suddenly down the sidewalk
Comes the truth
In the form of a girl
Into 35 rue Notre Dame des Champs
Hey, is this the closest place
To where I want to be? Noël says
A joke is a joke. Come on, take
The box out. We don't
Quarrel, actually. B-17,
Farewell.

Two girls
Ana and Svenita
One of them
Is studying Arabic
What do I care?
The water glass is on
The Frigidaire
An American patent
A big heavy white bird
Flown from America
To here in France
I place my
Hand on Svenita's
Shoulder—
And the white flag
Of seasonal peripheries
Is scuttering everybody
To dunk back into the beds
Whereupon suddenly
All the same

It is a force (Yeats)
A catastrophe (Quevedo)
A chase (Montgomery)
A flower (Keats)
And beauty with a graveled mace has done
I see her at the airplane counter—South

Outstretched—North-wind rubberband?
Is it religious
To dream of the Southern Cross?
The band is playing, the Riviera has walks—
Whiteness today is our special, I mean of the sun—

In Nice upon the Walk attired in whitest
Silks and linens men and women went
Forwards and backwards in what seemed the brightest
Light to earth the sun had ever sent
Baking the sidewalks white, with an excitement
Felt only insofar as it was meant
To be the belt of paradise around one,
When, striped with thirst, one stops beside a fountain

The white roadway shines ahead it is
A sidewalk! In front
Beyond the windows' cou-cou-cou. I grow up
Into these shades, white and referenced
Of slender wood, somebody being always nervous about the time

Tremulous and capsizing fresh stone in the hall
On which you stumble—I catch you—
Today is seeming, in truth, a beautiful day
"You use that word too much" is a seeming
Indifferent, well maybe not so much, distinction
And the restaurant of the animals, door, is hay
Which to them smells "beautiful" and I am out my door "beautiful"
Day, sitting on the speech stump and worrying about the door—

Comatose amidon
Hand held and then released
Stairways
Always on the edge of
Seeming to want
The book opened and then the book

What is outside—cars, windows
Abroad what is inside—aimlessness, scarves,
Or, in another view, thoughts,
First smell of cattle over the evening
The burning (hot was used as an ashtray) shell

Later evenings—it was already summer
Reflections of the outside
Taking the inside's form and making it follow

A grassiness is bursting in the light
That makes it seem more than autonomous.
A good trick, then, to be phoning. My (our) "nerves."
Visiting, it's vicious, it's long-gone time.
I walk down this sidewalk it's frappant it takes where you are

Blossomingness—and she says, You have a car, yes
We hot car have legs, shine cross, then, there
High nothingness elevator my clock "re-spaced"
Tables away, plates away, gavels away, the nothing
And something in a yellow dress while
Someone in a blue and white shirt bends over
Something made of wood with four legs. I hadn't read
Marcabru yet. Oh an
Old friend's poem, encased in a letter,
Smelling of soap,
January morning, while a truck goes past.
A word decelerated from a window. Type
Evaporated
From a newspaper. *Daily Cross.* Done
Nineteen forgotten
Centuries
Of progress, red
Shoes, white linen
The Russians are doing an experiment
In painting. Summer
Collapsed on summer like a clothes-
Pin snap on a piece of clothes.

He asked her to dance.
So Larry and I go to look at the picture
Of Z. Z. de A. pinching the nipple of Bambambomba

Dominique Celestin qu'en sais-je with the little briny street
The painters lived on, whiter than a mule of hay
And vigorous in a blank unquestioning manner

It was sixty-five degrees
Out. Perfect ("perfect") weather.

All right, let's get married. Will you marry me?
This marriage is done. I want you back.
You never had me. Bringing the suitcases around.
Bringing them back. Sitting in the Hotel de Fleurus.
This floor is sandy. With you,
The best way is to separate today

I couldn't then—Olivier says Think it over!
But lost for that holiday. It stings, it
The Greek art collection, walking
Sideways, it was hard to keep up. The greatest person ever to come in
This restaurant. Her fine-boned person
And rouge et le lipstick all around
For all anyone ever understood
About it, really

John said The hula hoop identity
Of all these straw persons interests me
Then finally he was promoted
To laugh at the bar of heaven We poets are the Jews of Literature
Scamping around at me—Especially you!

I can't believe you're doing this—not insured
Not protected by anything, I felt her hand, wristbone, of my own
The Danilova equivalent, a starring baggage—then chair
Being have brought out upon the sidewalk
The bed that Dan raved about checks in with and this suit

Printed in grey letters, on the top of the fire escape,
Look at it Guillevic said, look, look at it!
Proof that we live forever, or at least in a magazine!
For example, and we look at it. Place it
On top near the coffee, well, that's all right

Going out into the flawed light meter
Of a desky October day
Cutting it so closely as she did with the card
Then off cut a little bit of her hair top too with the names
I don't know where to put the import actually
Outside or in

Listen, I'm up—electric hand
Go to my shoe and bind it to those feet
That walked around the wings
I was unwrapping
Profit from it smiling what where is it

Hidden underneath South winds tabletop
Centered on
Each of us, face gone
To wondering silently about
A day and its intimate whether
I should have been in the storm with her or not

Alone without shoes she is bending half the time
Morning comes but safely takes away its wild go-out-
To-get-me-something spared by the future Palatine
Formed which the weeds shout. Two girls, one acting lazy
And the other hooking around, then S. X. comes to the door
The ballet is grazing, across that marble floor
In such time we sectioned off a daisy—I said
On time, but admit today's a failure
Because of its electricity

Drunk in my white suit at Noël Lee's house
Taking a shower I thought
Essences, never seeing anything at all
So wrapped around me as collectedness
And then (she) going to sleep, bearing me goes up
To future sky, post-Cubism, nineteen sailing nought
To cure all that
Dashing, but it won't work. Summer französisch. Your love.
Gunshot. These partings from some
Time

Flowers umphing around
And scratch to this to that for
I and the skirt the body sums
Keeping and smiling up
To walk

It's in the goat
And in the footnote.
It lamps what is not to come
As well as what is, a bannister of bones and a hat.
It felt like forever.
It feels "interrogating flat." It feels shown.
Vanning about and straggling. Why is it so unknown?
Getting out of the car and going back.